MACY McMILLAN
AND THE
Rainbow Goddess

·MACY

McMILLAN·
AND THE
Rainbow
Goddess

by Shari Green

pajamapress

First published in Canada and the United States in 2017

Text copyright © 2017 Shari Green.
This edition copyright © 2017 Pajama Press Inc.
This is a first edition.
10 9 8 7 6 5 4 3 2 1

www.pajamapress.ca   info@pajamapress.ca

 Canada Council   Conseil des arts
for the Arts   du Canada

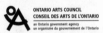 ONTARIO ARTS COUNCIL
CONSEIL DES ARTS DE L'ONTARIO
an Ontario government agency
un organisme du gouvernement de l'Ontario

The publisher gratefully acknowledges the support of the Canada Council for the Arts and the Ontario Arts Council for its publishing program. We acknowledge the financial support of the Government of Canada through the Canada Book Fund (CBF) for our publishing activities.

Library and Archives Canada Cataloguing in Publication

Green, Shari, 1963-, author
    Macy McMillan and the rainbow goddess / Shari Green.
ISBN 978-1-77278-033-8 (hardcover).--ISBN 978-1-77278-017-8 (softcover)
    I. Title.
PS8613.R4283M33 2017   jC813'.6   C2016-906085-3

Publisher Cataloging-in-Publication Data (U.S.)

Names: Green, Shari, 1963-, author.
Title: Macy McMillan and the Rainbow Goddess / by Shari Green.
Description: Toronto, Ontario, Canada: Pajama Press, 2017. |Summary: "Deaf sixth-grader Macy expects disaster when she is sent to help her elderly neighbor Iris, who doesn't know sign language, pack for a move to an assisted-living home. To her surprise, Iris soon becomes a firm friend who helps Macy face her own upcoming move, into the home of her mother's soon-to-be husband and two young stepsisters" — Provided by publisher.
Identifiers: ISBN 978-1-77278-017-8 (paperback) | 978-1-77278-033-8 (hardcover)
Subjects: LCSH: Deaf children – Juvenile fiction. | Stepfamilies – Juvenile fiction.| BISAC: JUVENILE FICTION / Family / Stepfamilies. | JUVENILE FICTION / Social Themes / Special Needs.
Classification: LCC PZ7.G744Mac |DDC [F] – dc23

Illustration—Jacqueline Hudon-Verrelli
Cover design—Rebecca Buchanan
Interior design and typesetting—Rebecca Buchanan, and Martin Gould / martingould.com

Manufactured by Friesens
Printed in Canada

Pajama Press Inc.
181 Carlaw Ave., Suite 207, Toronto, Ontario Canada, M4M 2S1

Distributed in Canada by UTP Distribution
5201 Dufferin Street, Toronto, Ontario Canada, M3H 5T8

Distributed in the U.S. by Ingram Publisher Services
1 Ingram Blvd., La Vergne, TN 37086, USA

For Jesse

Our house on Pemberton Street
with the red front door
wildflower garden out back
window seat just right for reading
has a *For Sale* sign jammed
in the front lawn.
It's the ugliest thing
I've ever seen.

I drop my school stuff
in my room
zip to the kitchen
mix up some chocolate milk
and gulp it down
hoping to make my escape
before Mom even knows
I'm home.

No
such
luck.

From the corner of my eye
I see her in the doorway
waving
to get my attention.

I turn to face her.
      How was your day?
she asks
in sign language.

I sign back
tell her it was fine
until I saw the *For Sale* sign again.
      That ruins my day
      every day.

She rolls her eyes
which doesn't seem
like a very *mom* thing
to do.

A moment later
she pulls out her phone
frowns at the screen
uses her free hand to sign
      It's work—one minute.

I set my glass in the sink
wait
while Mom talks
probably explaining computer stuff
to a confused client.

      Sorry
she says
when the call's done.

After tucking the phone away
she touches her thumb to her forehead
then to her other thumb—*remember*—
and already I know
what she's going to say.

> **Remember**
> **to work on the centerpieces.**

I'm supposed to make centerpieces
for the reception
—a tea in the church hall
after the wedding next month.
I don't get why anyone needs centerpieces
to stare at while they drink tea
after a bride
who is my mother
and a groom
who is not my dad
say *I do*.
Besides, shaping ribbon
candles
fake flowers
into something other than a mess
is not my specialty.
My skills are more
bookish.
I can hide out
read past my bedtime
get lost in a story
like a pro.

But the poppies are blooming
I say
with a long look
out the kitchen window.
Growing wildflowers
is another of my specialties.
**I should be there
to witness their grand opening.**

Mom glances outside
to my corner of the backyard
where fuzzy green stems hold buds
round and ripe
a few already open
crimson petals fluttering
in the breeze.

Fine
she says.
**Go. But don't put off this job
much longer. It'll be June
before you know it.**

I hug her quick
turn to leave.
She taps my shoulder.

What now?

You still need to pack too.

Right.
I'm thinking if I never pack my stuff
I can't move to a new house
with a new stepfamily
ever.

Mr. Tanaka tells the class

about our final project
of sixth grade.
I glance at him long enough
to see his excitement
—how much he thinks
we'll love this—
but it's still going to mean
homework
so I don't expect we'll love it
as much as he does.

I turn my focus to Ms. Eklund
my interpreter
who signs everything
Mr. Tanaka says.

Ms. Eklund fingerspells
    g-e-n-e-a-l-o-g-y
says it means where we came from
or rather
who we came from
ancestors
family history
family tree
as if we're all leaves

on a big old maple.
We have to trace our roots
make a chart or poster
present our work clearly
and thoughtfully.
We can include stories
from different generations
some photographs
if we have them.

I've got a feeling
my project
will be bare
a family tree
with only a few leaves clinging
to the branches.
Besides Mom and me
there's Uncle Caleb
in Saskatoon
and my Gran and Grampa
in Detroit.
That's it
for family.

**Do you even know
your dad's name?**
Olivia asks me at recess
while a bunch of us sixth-graders
kill time
at the edge
of the school playground.

**How on earth
are you going to create
a decent project?**

Olivia's been my best friend
since I came to Hamilton Elementary
in second grade
transferring
from Braeside, the School
for the Deaf.
She lives only a block
from me
and of all the kids in my class
she knows the most sign language.
But sometimes
she says something dumb
—like asking if I know
my father's name—
and the other kids
laugh.

I know
I shouldn't let it bug me
tug me
tie me
in angry knots
but controlling my temper
is not
one of my specialties.

My hand snaps closed
at my mouth, signing
    Shut up!
And before I can think
I add
    I hate you!
and my stupid foot
jabs into the pebbly dirt
beside the playground
sprays tiny stones
at her shins.

My stomach clenches.
I want to undo the last minute
dust off her shoes
her shins
smooth the ground
take back the words
my hands hurled.

Olivia's face flames pink
eyes fill
and she turns away.

After recess
Mr. Tanaka appears at my desk.
He may not know
much sign language
but somehow he knows
to give me detention.

By the time
I'm allowed to leave class
Olivia
is long gone.

I spoke to Ms. Gillan this morning

says Mom.
**She could really use a hand
packing up her books
before she moves.**

Ms. Gillan lives next door.
There's a *For Sale* sign
in her lawn too
but somehow
it doesn't look as nasty
as the one in ours.

Mom says
**I told her
you'd be glad to help.**

Me?

**I haven't even packed
my own books yet.**

Mom's face says she's fully aware
of my lack of packing
and not exactly happy
about it.

If you're not
getting your own things in order
she says
you may as well
help with hers.

This is worse than detention.
I barely know Ms. Gillan.
She's old
and crabby
and she doesn't sign.

I'll pack my things, I promise!

Yes, you will.
But you'll also help Ms. Gillan.
Now go.
She's expecting you.

I wilt like a daisy
snapped off by the stem
and left
in the afternoon heat.

Mom's expression softens.
It's only a few boxes of books
she says.
It shouldn't take long.

I trudge back outside
cross the lawn

to Ms. Gillan's house
reach up to flick a maple leaf
on the branch above me
as I pass.
I ring the buzzer
and wait.

Ms. Gillan opens the door
peers down at me
pale blue eyes set deep
in her lined face.
Her white hair protrudes
in wispy waves
reminding me
of a dandelion gone to seed.
After she lets me in
I follow her
to the living room
stop
stare.

Two walls are orange
bright
bold
nasturtium orange.

The other two walls
are completely hidden
by towering
shelves
of books:

shelves and   shelves and   shelves and
shelves and   shelves and   shelves and
shelves and   shelves and   shelves and
shelves and   shelves and   shelves and
shelves and   shelves and   shelves and
shelves and   shelves and   shelves and
shelves.

A few boxes of books?

I'm going to be here
forever.

I realize Ms. Gillan
has been talking.
I shake my head
shrug a little
hope she'll try again
with fewer words.
She does.
She points to a pile of cardboard
beside a floral recliner
—flattened boxes.
When she hands me a roll of wide tape
I understand.
I bend
fold
unfold
try again
until the cardboard becomes
a box shape.

I tear off a strip of tape
that stickstoitself
in a crumpled mess
cut another strip
manage to tape closed
the bottom
of the box.

I'm taping up the third box
when my nose wrinkles
at the stink
of permanent marker.
Ms. Gillan is writing on box number one
in thick black letters
KEEP
She picks up the second box
writes
DONATE
waits for me to hand her
box number three
writes
RECYCLE

I glance at the two walls of shelves
wonder how many more boxes
I'll need to make.

When I look back at Ms. Gillan
she's breathing hard
like she just ran laps
in gym class

but there was only bending
writing
and the stink
of marker.
She sinks into an armchair.

Now I know
why she can't pack
her own books.

I bring a stack from the first shelf
set it on the floor
near the boxes
hold up one book after another
for Ms. Gillan's directions.

1. keep
2. donate
3. donate
4. donate
5. keep

A slip of paper falls
from book number six.
I reach for it—a receipt
ink faded away
like it melted
right into the paper
leaving only
a faint stain.

I hold it over the RECYCLE box
raise my eyebrows in question.
Ms. Gillan clamps onto my forearm
drawing it close so she can see
the receipt in my hand.
She peers intently
releases my arm
takes the paper
and kisses it.

Seriously.
She kisses
an old receipt.

Then she starts talking
eyes ablaze
words words
words words
mouth moving faster
than I can follow.
I shake my head
and the words
stop.
The light in Ms. Gillan's eyes dims
as she leans back
into the chair cushion.
She points to the sixth book
still in my hand
—*Les Misérables.*
Is it even in English?

I watch her lips form the word.
"Keep," she says
which I'd already guessed.

Olivia didn't speak to me

look at me
acknowledge I exist.
I sat with Julianne and Emma
at lunch
but whenever I signed to them
they pasted on big smiles
so fake
nodding
pretending they understood
but I might as well have had a conversation
with my sandwich.
I'm glad they sat with me
but it's times like this
I really miss Desi
and my other friends
at Braeside
—kids I can really talk to.

Now that school's done
for the day
I should be researching
my family tree project

but I have to help Ms. Gillan
who stopped
trying to talk to me yesterday
after the book-six incident
like it was suddenly
too much trouble
not worth it
and I'm feeling more and more
like a dried-up
all-alone-on-my-branch
leaf.

I ring the bell
wait
wait
wait
until Ms. Gillan opens the door
wearing scarlet pants
and an orange blouse
as bright
as her walls.

She leans against the door frame
catching her breath.
When she's ready
I head for the living room
but she stops me
leads me down the hall
to the kitchen

slow as a fuzzy caterpillar
making its way
along the fence top.
She points to a chair
so I pull it out from the table
sit down
wonder
what I'm in for.

She sets a glass of lemonade
on the table
hands me a sheet of paper
filled
with handwriting.

After giving me a nod
Ms. Gillan pours another glass
of lemonade
sits across from me
sips
waits
while I read.

I'd left my favorite novel on the bus.
I knew the ending well, of course, and yet

I bought another copy in a shop,
got chatting with the man who worked the till.

He loved the book, it seemed, as much as I.
"It's closing time," he said, neck blushing pink.

Perhaps I'd like to get some tea with him—
the small café next door? I said I would.

We took a window seat and talked for hours
of Jean Valjean, Cosette, a priest who dared

to offer second chances—oh! such fun
to speak of books, redemption, hope. The world

went by on rainy streets outside. Next day
I found my way back to the little shop.

"He's gone back east," the owner said of him.
"His father passed. He'll have to help his mom.

I don't expect him back for quite some time
—if ever." Then I stepped outside and paused

beneath the bookshop sign: A Storied Life—
took in the lines and swirls of the words

and stored away the memory of when
I'd left my favorite novel on the bus.

Was this the story
with all the words words words?
The sixth-book story
from yesterday?

I rush to the living room
find the KEEP box
grab *Les Misérables* and return
to the kitchen.

I tap a finger on the book cover
then on the first line
of Ms. Gillan's story.
I sign
      Favorite book?
move my mouth
in the shape of the words
hoping
she'll understand.
She smiles.

"Yes. My favorite book."

      And the man?
I ask
pointing at the handwritten words
on the paper.

"I never saw him again."

I find a pen
write on the back
of Ms. Gillan's paper.

We should find him!

What an adventure
that could be.
But she's shaking her head
doesn't want to search.

She takes the pen
from my hand.

> *It was years ago. Decades.*
> *That story had the right ending*
> *even if it was a little sad.*

For just a moment
Ms. Gillan reminds me
of an autumn leaf
just as alone
as I am.

Saturday after lunch
I dress in my soccer uniform
find Mom at her desk
nibbling the end
of a pen.
She looks up from her day-planner
eyes widen
at the sight of me.
> **You have a game today?**

I have a game
every
Saturday.

A mix of guilt and panic flashes
across her face.
> **I've got a meeting**
> **with the florist.**
> **Maybe Alan can take you?**

Her expression says this is a question
like, would I mind?
only it's not really a question
because what other option
is there?
The game starts
in a half hour.

She grabs her phone
while I go fill my water bottle.
Even though I hate
missing games
I kind of hope Alan
is busy.

Nope.
He and the twins
will be right over.

The drive to the field
goes pretty much as I expected
me in back, sandwiched
between Bethany and Kaitlin
curly ponytails bobbing
both girls in constant motion
—more than you'd think possible
when strapped down
by seatbelts—
patting my arms
to get my attention
for a million questions
I can't decipher
and Alan
glancing at me in the rear-view mirror
awkwardly signing parts of sentences
with one hand
while he drives with the other.

It's a relief
to dash across the pitch
meet up with my team
even though my coach taps his wrist
reminding me
I'm almost late.

I'm the second-worst player
on our team
because I get distracted
by buttercups
blooming
on the field
in danger of being trampled
by multitudes of cleats.
I'm paying attention today, though
when Olivia searches
for someone to pass to.
I'm open
but Olivia kicks the ball
to Jennifer Blister.
Jennifer
is the first-worst player
on the team.
Last game
she scored on our own team.
Twice.
She receives the ball
turns
boots it hard.

One thing you have to admit
about Jennifer:
she's got a powerful
kick.

The ball flies through the air
shooting off
toward the sidelines
and right
toward
Bethany and Kaitlin.
Bethany ducks.
Kaitlin
is too late
flings up her arms
to protect herself.
The ball
hits Kaitlin hard
before dropping to the ground
beside her.

Bethany grabs the ball
marches
onto the field
throws it
at Jennifer's feet.
She's hollering something
her tiny six-year-old self
giving Jennifer Blister
what-for.

Kaitlin's finger is bent weird
disgusting
not at all the shape
it's meant to be.
We have to go to the hospital
and I have to miss
the rest
of my game.

All of us pile
into Alan's car.
Kaitlin leans against me
head on my shoulder
sniffy nose probably smearing
on my soccer jersey.

Ugh.

She's cradling her wrecked hand
in her lap
tears glistening
on her face.
I put my arm around her
pat her shoulder
because I don't know what else
to do.

Alan parks at the hospital
leads us inside
white walls
tile floor
the smell of disinfectant
hanging
in the halls.
After forever
Kaitlin's finger is X-rayed
splinted
taped to the next not-broken finger.
She holds up her hand
proud
a hard-won souvenir
of her adventure.

Next stop: ice cream.
Alan buys sundaes for us
and we slide onto the plastic benches
of a booth.
The twins lift their bowls
tap their soft-serve twists together
—*cheers!*—
in serious danger
of losing the whole lot
in their laps.

They laugh
make a mess
never
stop
moving
and Alan does nothing
about it.
Just grins.

I slip up to my room

slide a book from the shelf
jot a note
and stick it
on the cover

> *My favorite book.*
> *It's about a mouse*
> *a princess*
> *and soup.*

Then I head to Ms. Gillan's house.
Maybe this isn't a good idea
but maybe
it is.
Maybe she's not as crabby
as I thought.
She might just be
lonely.
And I *know*
she likes books.

When I get there
I hand her the book.

She reads my note
flips the book over
peers
at the back cover.

"Soup?" she says.

I shrug
smile
wait.

When she looks up again
I tell her
> **You can borrow it**
> **if you want.**
But I don't think
she understands
my signing.
She walks slowly
to the living room
reaches for a pocket-size notebook
leaf-green cover
a pen
tucked in its spiral binding.
She presses it into my hand
and waits.
I take the pen
open the notebook
fresh clean pages
write

Would you like to borrow
my favorite book?

She lights up.
"Yes, please," she says
and then her mind
seems to wander
lost
in a daydream.
I do that too
when I have a good book
in hand.

I reach out tentatively
touch her arm.
She turns her attention to me.
    Ms. Gillan? You okay?

She taps her chest
with her index finger
then slowly
deliberately
shapes her hand
—fingerspelling

    i-r-i-s

then she says
"Call me Iris."

I jot in the notebook

How did you learn
to fingerspell?

She nods toward a desk
at the back of the room
a computer
sitting front and center.
She Googled it?
That's actually kind of
cool.

I write again

So...Iris?
Like the flower?

I make the sign for *flower*
fingertips together
touch the sides of my nose.

Her mouth drops open
eyes pop wide.
"Certainly not!" she says.

Okaaay.
Not
like the flower.

She strides to the shelves
surprising me
with her speed.
She searches
for just a moment
pulls out a paperback
with black and gold cover.
She flips through
stops
stabs a finger
at the page
and shoves the book
toward me.

I peer at the spot
she indicated.

Iris, Goddess of the Rainbow.

She's named after a goddess?
Wow. I suppose
if I'd been named after a goddess
I'd be proud of that.
But I was named after one of my mother's
wild friends

(back in the days
when she had wild friends).

Wild Friend Macy won the coin toss
in the hospital delivery room.
If the dime had landed heads
rather than tails
I'd be named after Wild Friend Duckie
instead.
I'm not sure the kids at school
would ever
let me live that down.

Iris presses the book into my hands
so I take it
sink cross-legged onto the carpet
and read about a rainbow goddess
a messenger for the gods
traveling
by rainbow.

When I hold out the book
to give it back
she says, "Donate."

It seems like an important book
to her
but maybe
she thinks someone else
needs to read it.
Into the box
it goes.

I retrieve the notebook
ask what might be
a cheeky question
but
I honestly want to know
what she'll say.

*Do you ever deliver messages
from the gods?*

I keep a straight face
waiting for her answer
even though the idea of Iris
riding a rainbow
passing notes
from Zeus or Hera
makes a giggle rise up
inside me.

A hint of a smile
appears on her face.
Not a laughter-coming smile
but the kind you get
when you're remembering heart things
like quiet times
with your mom
or the moment you knew
a certain someone
was going to be your friend.

Iris takes the pen
and we write notes
back and forth.

I used to, yes.
But I'm rather past that now.

What sort of messages
did you send?

Important ones.
I sent them
through cookies.

As I read her reply
my eyebrows shoot up
but Iris closes the notebook
tucks it beside her
on the chair
points
at a book-lined wall.

We've hardly made a dent
in the sorting
and packing.

I tape together a new box
before gesturing at one wall of books
then the other

letting my expression ask
why she has
so very many books.

"I love books," she says.

That's obvious enough.
But still
hasn't she heard
of libraries?

Once again
she flips to a fresh page
in the notebook.

If you love something
you should love it extravagantly.

My gaze flicks to the painted walls
her shirt
the cushion on the couch.
I write back

So if you love the color orange?

She reads it and laughs
head tipped back
mouth open
like I've said the funniest thing.

"Then love it extravagantly,"
she says, facing me
so I can see her speak.

On a fresh page
I write

And if you love books?

If you love books
read a great many books.
If you love to sing
sing loudly
and often.
Whatever you do
do it with all your heart.

I think about my garden
about collecting seeds
nurturing plants
discovering the flowers
that love my yard best
spending my free time nestled
between daisies and fireweed
and I understand
about Iris
having so many books.

What I don't understand
is what's so bad
about being named
after a flower.

Ms. Eklund interprets

as Mr. Tanaka reminds us
of our project
says that by now
we should have a good start.

I don't even have
an idea.

I glance around the class
hoping for a glimpse
a hint of how others
are tackling the project
but kids are pushing back chairs
moving away
from their desks.
I've missed something
whip around
to Ms. Eklund.

Time for gym
she says.
Outside.

For gym class
we're doing track.
After leading us on a warm-up run
around the block
—which we didn't need
because it's crazy hot out here—
Mr. Tanaka lets us pick
sprints
or endurance.

When it's time for the 100 meter
I line up on the track.
Olivia and I find ourselves
right next to each other
without even planning it.
It's natural to be together
side by side
peas in a pod
peanutbutterjelly
but
Olivia moves
so there are two other kids
between us.

Mr. Tanaka lifts a whistle
to his mouth
raises his hand
in the air
so he can signal me at the same moment
he blows the whistle.

His hand comes down
and we all run
shooting off down the track
squinting
in the sunshine.

Usually I'm pretty fast.

Today
I come in last.

Olivia walks off the track
without a glance
in my direction.

How is she supposed to forgive me
if she won't look
if she can't see me saying
I'm sorry?

I step out the back door
cross the yard to my garden
pull a few weeds
and wave away a bumble bee
that seems to think
I'm a flower.
It finds the poppies
then weaves
toward the fireweed.
I almost wish
it would come back
keep me company
because this afternoon
even being with a bee
might feel better
than being alone.

A deep breath
fills my nose
my lungs
my whole self
with the sweetness
of wild roses.
It makes an ache
grow in my chest.

I collect the bits of chickweed
I've gathered
drop them
in the compost heap
brush off my hands
and head inside.

In the living room
I log on to the computer
message Desi
to see if she can video chat.
Her reply pops up
right away.

Sorry—leaving for swim club.
Maybe tomorrow?

Lately it seems
she has less time for me
and I have less time
for her.
Desi's parents still see my mom
every week
—support group
for signing practice.
Lots of parents don't bother
but Mom
has been going faithfully
ever since I lost my hearing
way back
when I was four.

Who knew meningitis
would change our lives
so much?

I log off
check the clock
glad to discover it's time
to pack books
for Iris.

Iris greets me at the door
dressed in an orange tee shirt
pink pants
lavender apron
colors that work great
for gardens
and sunsets
so why not
for a rainbow goddess?

Her kitchen is warm
the air heavy
with the scent of sugar
giving me the feeling I've stepped
into a gingerbread house.

Iris holds out a plate
of enormous ginger cookies
each one nearly as big
as my face.
I remember what she wrote
in the notebook
about being all in

and I imagine her saying
if you're going to bake cookies
bake enormous cookies
bake excellent cookies
bake the very best cookies
you can bake.
I take one
from the plate
bite into sugar-sprinkled goodness.
A hint of crunch on the outside
disappearing into a chewy middle
of spicy sweetness
possibly the best
cookie
ever.

Delicious
I say
signing with my non-cookie hand.

Iris smiles
reaches into her apron pocket
pulls out the notebook
and pen.

> *If you bake them*
> *with extravagant love in your heart*
> *they turn out*
> *just a wee bit magical.*

Magic?

"They send messages," Iris says.

She wasn't kidding
about sending messages
in cookies?

I turn over the cookie in my hand
look for a slip of paper
like you'd find in fortune cookies.
Iris touches my arm
extends the notebook
so I can read
what she's added.

That's my job, isn't it?
Passing on messages from the gods?

I set down my cookie
take the notebook
write

I thought you didn't do that
anymore.

It's been a while.

She lifts a small metal box from the counter
flips back the hinged lid.
The box is stuffed
with recipe cards.

Iris riffles through them
pulls out a card
stained
with a greasy splotch.
It's the recipe
for chocolate chunk cookies.

She sets the card on the counter
writes in the notebook

> *Chocolate chunk cookies say*
> *"You'll be okay."*

Another card

> *Oatmeal cookies say*
> *"You're strong enough...you can do this."*

A third card

> *Peanut butter cookies send joy*
> *and laughter.*

And finally the recipe
for sugar & spice cookies
—the ones on the plate.

> *These ones whisper*
> *"You are loved, you belong."*
> *It's the most important message*
> *of all.*

I take the pen from her hand
ask if those are messages
from the gods.

*I don't know
but if they aren't
they should be.*

I nod
but I still don't understand
how a cookie
can send a message.
But then, after I finish the last bite
of the enormous
sugar & spice cookie
head for the living room
kneel on the worn carpet
hold up book after book
for Iris to decide about
I notice something.

I'm comfortable here
with this old lady
who doesn't even sign
who wears something orange
every single day
and thinks the gods
send their messages
through her.

Maybe they do.

Something prickles
at my nose
making it twitch.
I lift my chin
sniff the air.
Iris's brow furrows
then her eyes widen
hand slaps over her mouth
other hand pointing pointing pointing
frantic
and I know
what the smell is.

I run to the kitchen
find a potholder
yank open the oven.
Smoke billows out
stinging my eyes.
I wave it away
pull out the pan
of six
extra-large
blackened
cookies.

After turning off the oven
opening the window that faces my house
to air the place out
I find Iris in the doorway
hands over her ears.

It's just the cookies

I say
but she must not understand
because she's shaking
a look of confusion on her face
that is not at all
like her usual self.

When she doesn't move from the doorway
I walk through the haze
put my hand on her arm
tell her again
it's okay.

Behind her
the hallway fills with light.
The front door is open
my mom hurrying
toward us.
She glances side to side
like she's looking for something.
Then she's in the kitchen.
She grabs a dishtowel
waves it under the smoke detector.

Iris uncovers her ears
sinks onto a kitchen chair
eyes downcast
hands trembling
in her lap.

My mom talks to her
calms her
gives her a hug.

Later at home, I ask Mom
why Iris was so upset.

It was partly the smoke alarm
Mom says.
It's very loud.
I could hear it
from the backyard.

And partly what else?
I ask.
What did she tell you?

Mom hesitates.

She said, *I could've started a fire*
could've burned down
the house.

She said, *I can't even bake*
anymore.

We're painting "still life" in art

a bowl of apples
a vase of flowers.
I'm not a fan
of art class.
The best thing about it
is sharing my workspace
with Olivia.

Today Olivia shares a table
with Montana
which sounds like she's sharing
with an entire state
but it's just this one girl.
Montana's mostly nice
but today it seems she's in cahoots
with Olivia
working together
to leave me out.
They cup a hand around their mouth
when they talk
so I can't guess
what they're saying.
They link arms
march to the supply cupboard
as a team.

I feel myself getting riled up
heated up
ready
to burst
but that would only make Olivia glad
she's with Montana
instead of me.
I study the scuffed floor tiles
until they're finished
at the cupboard
then steal across the room
grab paints and paper
for myself
zip to my table
bend over my work
begging the time to go quickly.

I don't even look up
to consider the apples
or the vase
on Ms. Kovalchuk's desk
—just draw my still life
from memory
trying to create sunflowers
like the ones by Van Gogh
in a poster on the wall.
My flowers don't look like his
or like the ones standing tall
by our back fence

but drawing them eases out
a little of my anger.
Art's weird that way.

I sneak a glance
at Olivia
just as she sneaks a glance
at me.
She looks away
after a moment
but the moment is long enough
to give me hope.

Maybe
just maybe
our friendship isn't 100 percent
doomed.

A tiny plastic hula dancer
wiggles her hips
on the next bookshelf.
She wiggles right into a KEEP box
and Iris writes three pages
in her notebook
about her hairdresser, Elaine.
She tells me how Elaine fell in love
in Hawaii
and didn't come back home.
She sent the hula dancer to Iris
some years ago.

> *Elaine had a hard life here.*
> *I'm so pleased she found love—*
> *there's no greater happiness*
> *than to love and be loved.*

I turn to a new page
ask if Elaine
is her best friend.

"No," she says
and I wonder why, then, this souvenir
from Hawaii
belongs in the KEEP box.

As if she can read my mind
Iris scribbles another pageful.

> *Ever since Steven—the man in the bookshop—*
> *I make a point of connecting with people*
> *who come into my life*
> *because even if only for a moment*
> *their story connects with mine.*
> *That should mean something...*
> *even if there's no chapter in a café next door.*

When I look up from reading
she winks at me.

We sort for a while
until I come across a stack
of takeout menus
tucked between two books.

Recycle?
I ask
but she extends a hand
takes the pamphlets from me
shuffles through.
She keeps one aside
tosses the rest in the RECYCLE box.

Your favorite restaurant?
I ask
hoping she'll recognize the sign
for *favorite* and understand.

She grimaces.
"No," she says. "Terrible food."

> *But Kimmy the delivery driver*
> *is a lovely girl.*

She hands me Kimmy's menu
indicates where it should go
and the memories of terrible food
and a nice person
are stored within the pages
of a red hard-bound journal.

The foyer lights flash
indicating someone's rung
the doorbell.
Even though I've a clear view
of the front yard
from my window seat
I was so absorbed in my book
I didn't notice anyone
approach.
I clamber down
answer the door.

Iris stands on our front step
breathing hard
wearing an orange and white polka-dot
housedress.
Mom appears
ushers Iris
into the living room.

Once Iris is settled
on our couch
she reaches into the large pocket
of her dress
withdraws a book.
The Tale of Despereaux.

Mom interprets
as Iris and I talk.

      I finished this last night
Iris says.
      I wanted to return it
      in case you needed
      to read it.
      I know how it is
      with favorite books.

I take *Despereaux* from her
ask
      What did you think?

      I adored it, Macy.
      Thank you
      for sharing it with me.
      I should like to be
      as brave as that mouse
      as kind as that princess.

Iris stays for tea
with my mother.
I leave them visiting
settle on the window seat
open my book and slip
into the world
of a girl who calls herself
El Deafo.

Later, after Mom sees Iris home
she says
>**I don't know
>that she'll be up to coming
>to the wedding.**

Since I avoid wedding thoughts
as much as possible
it hadn't occurred to me
Iris might be there.

>**You invited her?**

>**Of course**
Mom says.
>**She's very dear.
>You know, she brought cookies
>for us
>the day we moved
>into this house.**

I think of last week's burned cookies
the smoke
Iris with her hands
over her ears.
Will she ever bake
again?

Mom says
>**We're fortunate to have her
>as a neighbor.**

She's right—we are.
I wonder where I got the idea
Iris was crabby
wonder why I never learned
her story.
I guess she never learned mine
either.
Even now
we barely know each other
and yet the thought
of a rainbow goddess
being present at my mother's wedding
somehow makes the whole
depressing
occasion
much more pleasant
to anticipate.

Glass jar
candle inside
flowers twisted
into a wreath that...

doesn't fit

around the base of the jar.

I know Mom gave me this job
to make me part
of the planning
as if it would make the wedding
the changing family
the moving-from-my-home
all seem like a great idea.
It's not working.

I untwist the fake flowers
reshape them
weave in lavender ribbon
and tie a bow.

Maybe this one's pretty good
—as good as it's going to get
anyway.

That's lovely
Mom says
even though
it's a bit lopsided.
**How many
have you finished?**

Um...

Just this one

**Macy! The wedding
is in two weeks! I need you to—**

Mom's hands freeze
mid-sign
drop to her side.
She walks past me
no explanation
strides across the living room
to peer out the front window.

What's happening?
I ask
and Mom says
Siren
points outside
where an ambulance
with lights flashing
slows

stops
right in front of Iris's house.
Mom and I rush
to Iris's yard.
The paramedics go inside
with their stretcher.
I want to follow
but Mom says no
so we wait on the lawn
my insides knotting up
as if weeds are twisting around my heart
my lungs
choking me.

When the paramedics finally reappear
Iris is strapped on the stretcher
some sort of mask
covering her mouth and nose.
Back door of the ambulance opens
stretcher bumps
rolling legs fold up
and Iris disappears
swallowed up inside.
The doors close
driver hops in the front
lights flashing again
and it drives away.

I've discovered

a universal truth.
School is ever so much harder
without a best friend.
I stumble through my red front door
drop my backpack
in the foyer
slump
on the sofa.
A moment later
chaos enters the room.
The twins are here.

Mom appears
arms laden
with board games.
She plunks them
on the coffee table
doesn't even ask
how my day went.

Alan's sitter bailed
she says.
Will you play with the girls?
I need some time
in my office.

**This morning I was at the hospital
visiting Iris
and now...**

She gestures toward Bethany and Kaitlin
who are spinning on the spot
then staggering about
dizzy.

You visited Iris?
I say.
Without me?

Her eyes bulge
like she's exasperated
can't believe
I'm missing the point.

I need to work
she says.
You're on duty.

She turns on her heel
vanishes
into her office.

I wave the twins over.
We're on our third game
of KerPlunk—marbles tumbling
down the clear plastic container
over and over—

when Mom marches into the room
scoops up marbles
container
plastic sticks
and plops them
in the box.

Maybe another game
she says
before striding back down
the hall.

I look at the twins
shrug.

"Too loud," Bethany explains
and the two of them
burst into giggles.

We play Candy Land instead
then find paper and crayons
draw pictures
until Alan appears with a bag
of takeout hamburgers.

I'm officially off duty.

Babysitting was actually okay
but I can't imagine
a lifetime of it

can't imagine such chaos
being permanent.

We gather at the table
eat our burgers and limp fries.
Alan jokes with Mom
the two of them
laughing together
not signing
as if I've suddenly become
invisible.

      What's so funny?
I say.

Mom turns to me
remnants of laughter
lingering
on her face.
      Alan's telling me
      about the record number of teeth
      he yanked out
      at work today.

Ick.

That's not even funny.
Dentist talk
is disgusting
should be banned
from the dinner table

but for some reason
Mom's laughing again.

As we're finishing dinner
Mom excuses herself
to take a phone call.
When she reappears at the table
her face is lit
eyes sparkling
lips pressed together
as if a huge grin
wants to spring
into place.

She signs for my benefit
but she's looking at Alan
when she spills the news.

**I got an offer
on the house!**

A sinking feeling
falls through me
like a stone
tumbling
landing
in my stomach.

Someone
wants to buy
our house.

I push my plate from me
slip away
close myself
in my bedroom.
If only I could convince Mom
to say no
to the offer
no to the wedding.
If only I could make her realize
this is all
a terrible
plan.

When Alan asked Mom
to marry him
it was like ivy
creeping into the garden
taking over
ruining everything.
I don't know how
to stop it.

My mind spins
insides quiver.
I need to quit thinking
about the house selling
my family
changing.

I pace the floor
pause to peer out the window
at my garden
pace again
crouch at the bookcase
can't decide
on a book.
I could do homework.
If I don't soon start
my genealogy project
Mr. Tanaka
will have a fit.

I pull out a sheet of paper
stare at it awhile
put it away.

Maybe tomorrow
I'll stumble
upon an idea.

Clear plastic tubing snakes

from Iris's nose
to a cylindrical tank
in a small, wheeled cart.

"Oxygen," she says
with a grimace
and a shrug
as if to say, *I hate it
but what can I do?*

She settles into her floral recliner
feet up
oxygen cart parked
beside her.
We sort two full shelves
of books.
Start on the next.

"I love that one," Iris says
when I hold up a small paperback.

She says more about the book
and I think she's telling me
she's read it

almost as many times
as *Les Misérables.*

Keep, then
I say
move toward the box.

She shakes her head.
"No," she says. "Donate."

I could never give away a book
I loved that much.

Iris jots in her notebook.

> *I know it inside out.*
> *I don't imagine*
> *I need to read it again.*

I crouch down
set *Anne of Green Gables* in the box
pause a moment
my fingertips lingering on the cover
—a redheaded girl
who looks about my age.

When I glance back at Iris
she says something
about passing it on
something
about a girl.

She speaks slowly
and even though I watch her lips
I have to piece together
what she's saying.

She wants to give the book
to a girl she knows?

I'm quite sure
she means me
but I point to myself
raise eyebrows
hope
because there's nothing better
than a well-loved book.
Iris nods, and I retrieve *Anne*
wonder what it is
about this story
that made an old woman love it
so much.

We need another DONATE box
so I pop out to her garage
lug cardboard into the living room
find the tape
and put together a box
including
the stinky ink
to label it.

When I finish
Iris hands me her spiral notebook.

> *I learned much from Anne—*
> *that the hard things in life*
> *sometimes turn out to be the very things*
> *that equip us for what comes next...*
> *that there's nothing so precious*
> *as a kindred spirit*
> *and a place to call home...*
> *that we need one another...*
> *that words are magical...*
> *and that it's possible—more than possible—*
> *to survive the depths of despair*
> *and come out strong.*

I look up from the page.
She learned all this
from one book?
I re-read her message
write back

> *Have you ever been*
> *in the depths of despair?*

"Oh yes," Iris says.

She struggles from her recliner
crosses the room
still tethered
to her oxygen tank.
She crouches to peer
at the bottom shelf
of a bookcase
picks through her collection
of hard-bound journals
slides a blue one
from the shelf.

We trundle down the hall
settle at the kitchen table
with a tin
of oatmeal cookies.
I remember their message
—*you're strong enough*
you can do this.

Iris opens the journal
turns pages gently
thoughtfully.
Many are filled
with her handwriting.
Others display bits
of this and that
—newspaper clippings
ticket stubs
photographs.

She slides the open journal
across the table
nods at the newsprint clipping
taped
to the page.

It's an obituary.

I skim the words
> *Thalia Gillan*
> *survived by her twin sister*
> *Iris.*

Iris has a twin?
Or, *had* a twin.
I swallow hard.
On the page next to the clipping
is a bulletin
from the funeral service.

I'm sorry
about your sister
I say.
I ask if she has more family
but she doesn't understand.
F-a-m-i-l-y
I fingerspell slowly
add a question mark
with my expression.

She shakes her head
sends me to the living room
for the brown journal.
I retrieve it
and she flips pages
shows me an old photo
of a man
in a military uniform
two dates underneath
—birth
and death.

Iris pulls the spiral notebook
from her apron pocket.

We were eleven when we lost him to the war.
Mother died soon after—perhaps of a broken heart.
Thalia and I were raised by our grandparents.
They're long gone, of course.
I still miss them
but I miss Thalia the most.

Yellow poster paper
permanent black marker
on my bedroom floor.
I draw a family tree chart
like the one Mr. Tanaka showed us
as an example.

It only takes a minute.
Most of the poster
is empty space
—I should've made my chart bigger.
I fill in names and birthdates
for my grandparents
but the lettering
is dreadful
—leaning one way
then the other
Grampa's last name squashed
to fit in a too-small space.
No wonder
Olivia's in charge of lettering
whenever we do projects
together.

My hand slips
fumbles the marker
leaving an ugly black streak
where my uncle's name
should be.

Argh!

In a flash
I slash black lines
across the stupid yellow poster
again
and again
destroying
my lousy project.

I tear it into quarters
shove
scrunch
smash the pieces
into the wastebasket.
Then I step back
take a breath
stare
at what I've done.

I feel sort of better
and sort of worse.

And I'll need a plan B.

I start daydreaming
aiming to think about a new way
to tackle my project
but my mind wanders
thinks about Iris instead.
My gaze lands
on the well-loved book
she gave me
reminding me
of the depths of despair
and I realize
Iris hasn't only been sharing books.
She's been sharing stories.

It seems like a good time
to tell her a story
of my own.

I glance around my room
hoping an idea
will leap up.
I pull out a sheet of paper
choose an orange fine-tip marker
don't know what to write
so I draw butterfly weed
—tiny blossoms in bunches
like clusters of stars
twinkling their way
along all four sides
of the page.

It's a bit like a wreath
which reminds me
of the centerpieces
which leads to another thought
I don't especially want
to think.
My tiny family
is changing.

I begin to write
orange words for Iris.

                    I
                  have
               to make a
             project for school
           telling my family history
              my family tree
         which is mostly Mom and me.
      Part of my heart wants more names
     to list on my project and part of it wants
   my family to stay exactly the way it is forever.
      My mom and I are a two-person team.
   I'm afraid adding a stepdad and two stepsisters
  will be like adding Jennifer Blister to our team and
 someone is going to get hit with the ball and knocked
out of the game—lose their place—and our team will never
           be the same. And yet two
                 is a very
                  small
                  team.

I uncap a green marker
add long skinny leaves
to the butterfly weed
then put down the pen
read my story
to myself.

Every time I try to get excited
about the wedding
and having a bigger family
something inside me closes up
like a fist grabbing tight to something
hanging on for dear life
so it doesn't get lost.

One person is important
on a team of two
but one can almost disappear
when there are five.

I fold the paper once
twice
three times
then tuck it in the drawer
of my nightstand.

The *For Sale* sign stuck

in our lawn
now has a *Sold* sticker
plastered across it.
I knew Mom accepted the offer
but that sticker
means I can't deny it
any longer.
We have to be out
by the end of June.
Mom says the timing
is perfect
but any time you lose your home
is the opposite
of perfect.

After the wedding
Mom and I are supposed to move
into Alan's house
which is the dumbest thing
I've ever heard.
Alan lives blocks and blocks
from Olivia's
—sixteen, to be exact.

His house has no garden
no window seat for reading
and everything
is painted beige.

Ugh.

Today we're there for dinner.
Family Night
Mom calls it
as if Alan and the twins
are actually related already.
When I come in the door
one twin grabs my left arm
the other twin grabs my right arm.
They lead me upstairs
through a doorway
into a drab office.
They're babbling away
pointing at me
the room
me again
then doing some crazy happy-dance.

My mom appears in the doorway.

  What do they want?
I say.

  **They're showing you
  your room.**

Huh?

**Alan's going to move his office
to the basement
and convert this
into a bedroom for you.**

I want my old room.
I can't imagine this puny office
being *home*.
The plain curtain hanging
at the small window
moves in the breeze.
I cross the room
lift the fabric
peer outside
at the smallest patch of grass
ever
and not a single
wildflower.
You can't call that
a backyard.

The twins
dash out of the room
and Mom tells me it's time
to make dinner.
Homemade pizza
my favorite,

but I'm not
going to admit that
to Alan.

In the kitchen
Bethany has already managed
to spill sauce on the counter
and Kaitlin
sends a red pepper bouncing
across the floor.
I shoot Mom a look
that says, *You want to be*
part of this?
She sends a look right back.
Behave yourself
or else.

Okay.
Make the best of this.
What did Iris say she learned
from that *Anne* book?
That good can come
out of hard things?
I'm going to get pizza
out of this chaos
so that's something.

I wash the battle-worn pepper
chop it into chunks
pile it on
over the pepperoni.

Enough
Mom tells me.
Not everyone loves peppers
as much as you do.

If I love red pepper
I should love it
extravagantly.

Mom raises her eyebrows
repeats the sign
Enough.

I toss another handful
onto the pizza
glare
at my mother.

Stop it
she says.
What's wrong with you today?

My signs are harsh
angry.
Nothing's wrong with me!
It's them!

From the corner of my eye
I see them watching
—Alan frowning
Bethany and Kaitlin
wide-eyed.
Remorse pricks at me
like thorns
but I can't help myself
words rush
from my hands.

    They don't like peppers
    don't like flowers
    don't even like color
    —look at this place!
    Beige everywhere!
    I can't live here.
    This isn't home. It will never
    be home.

If Olivia and I

were friends right now
I'd tell her how rotten I feel.
I'd tell her how my temper
got away from me at Alan's house
except it might remind her
of when my temper
got away from me
with her.
So instead
I'd tell her how I hate
that Alan and his pesky twins
are taking Mom away
from me.
I'd tell her how my family changing
scares me
makes me mad
mixes me up.

I did tell this story once—in orange marker.

The folded-up page I wrote for Iris
still hides
in my nightstand.

If I can't tell Olivia
I'll tell
a rainbow goddess.

I grab the paper
slip down the hall and outside
dart past the maple tree
and drop my story
through the mail slot
in Iris's front door.

I should be on my way next door
but after another
no-best-friend day
I need a book
and my spot
on the window seat.
I curl up
find my page
in the *Anne* book
read how desperately Anne hoped
for a best friend
—a bosom friend—
and instead of feeling better
an empty spot grows
inside me.

I finish the chapter anyway
(because how could I not?)
then I take my empty self
to empty more shelves
and fill
more boxes.

Iris hands me her spiral notebook
open to a page
she wants me to read.

Thank you for your story.
I myself am rather afraid of change
of letting go of the person I am
in favor of the person I'll become.
When you're in the midst of a good story
it's hard to remember
there are more wonderful tales to be told.

I look up
unsure what to say.
Iris points to the notebook
twitches her index finger
telling me
to flip the page.

How's your project going?

A short laugh bursts from me
making Iris smile.

Terrible
I say.

Maybe I'll try using the computer
for my project
so the lettering will at least
be legible.

If only Olivia and I
could work together.

If only Olivia...

>**Did you ever have a**
>**b-o-s-o-m f-r-i-e-n-d?**

I ask Iris
fingerspelling slowly. I'm not sure
what exactly *bosom* means
but it still seems
the perfect word
for what I need to say.

Iris smiles. "A kindred spirit, you mean?
Like Anne and Diana?"

Exactly like that.

Iris points to one of the bookshelves
where a small framed picture
rests
nudged up against colorful spines
—the Harry Potter series
all lined up.

She's read those?

I gesture at the familiar books
point at Iris
eyebrows raised.

"Wonderful stories," she says
then jiggles her fingers
directing me back
to the photo.

Five women
on a pier
arms around one another's shoulders
laughing.
I lift it from the shelf
hand it to Iris.
She presses it to her heart
pulls it away
smiles softly.

"The Five Firecrackers," she says
fingerspelling *firecrackers*.
"My, but we had wonderful
adventures."

Firecrackers?

"We were bold
cheerful
adventurous."
She points
at one of the women
says, "That's me."

A sadness comes over her then
settling on her like heavy rain
weighing down
a fawn lily.

Iris decides she's not up to sorting
so I slip away
return to *Anne*
and my window seat.
The empty spot feels raw
gnawing
at my insides.

After school the next day
I return to Iris's.
She sets a handwritten page
before me
hands me lemonade
offers cookies dusted
in cinnamon-sugar.

"Snickerdoodles," she tells me.

You baked again
I write on the edge of the paper
ignoring the story
for a moment.
    I wasn't sure...after last time.

"I didn't think I would," she says
"but with this—"
she taps the oxygen tube
turns over the story page
scrawls a note.

    This made me think
    I'd best do what I love doing
    while I've got the days left
    to do it.
    Mind you, I don't leave the kitchen now
    until I've triple-checked that the oven's off.

I help myself to a cookie
take a bite
then write
below Iris's note.

    I feel better already.

"You were sad?"
Iris asks.

I nod
take another bite.

This helps
I say
wondering if snickerdoodles
have magic cheering-up messages
baked into them.

Iris writes

> *I've found it's quite difficult to be sad
> while you're eating a cookie.*

Then she adds

> *What's bothering you?*

> *I miss my best friend.*

"Ah," she says
turning the paper over again
and tapping a finger
on her story.
"I understand."

When my sister died
my friends became family—
my true saving grace.
We shared our joys and sorrows
and loved extravagantly.

But now, besides me
only Marjorie is left.
She lives in Rosewood
and I visit each Thursday.
She often doesn't know me.

One crisp day last fall
I took my usual route
but oh, coming home—
coming home I lost my way.
I walked and walked for so long.

Wrong corners, wrong roads
wrong shops all along the way.
I was just like her—
Marjorie would do the same
before she moved into care.

Such terrible fear—
thought I'd never find my way
until finally:
Mr. Henderson's market—
something familiar to me.

He directed me
to Pemberton Street, and then
the flaming red leaves
of my dear old maple tree—
a beacon to lead me home.

Each week without fail
I gather up my courage
go to visit her—
bosom friend, true family—
but it scares me every time.

I can't imagine
being afraid to go see Olivia
—or worse
not being able to see her
because of moving
sixteen stupid blocks away
—or even worse than that
not being friends at all
because she never forgives me
for being mean.

I need
my best friend.
Everyone needs
their best friend.

Iris visits Marjorie on Thursdays
—tomorrow.
I snatch the paper
flip it over
write
                    I'll go with you
and hope
Mom will say okay.

That night as I'm lying in bed

I think of Iris
how her friends
were her family
and I think of those flaming leaves
calling her
helping her find her way
almost as if
they were whispering her story to her
reminding her
where home was.

Suddenly I know what to do
for my project.

Leaves
telling my story
—leaves for all the people
who feel like home
a family tree
that's about belonging and love
and being part of one another's stories
a family tree
that's not limited
to actual family.

I sleep well
so relieved
to finally have a plan.
I bound out of bed
eager to tell Olivia
—until I remember
she's not talking to me.
My energy vanishes
and I trudge to the kitchen
settle for telling Mom
instead.

What kind of leaves?
she asks
as I dump cereal into a bowl.

**Paper ones.
I'll write on them
list how each person fits
on my family tree.**

**That's not quite what Mr. Tanaka
will be expecting, is it?**

Grr.

This is why I'd rather be telling Olivia.

Olivia would love my idea
and even if she didn't

she'd be happy
I had one.
I'm about to tell Mom
I don't care
what Mr. Tanaka thinks of it
when her face brightens
abruptly.

Oh!
she says.
**You can paste them
on a giant poster-board tree!**

She obviously thinks
that's a brilliant idea
but I shake my head.
**The leaves
will be pages
of a book.**

Mom considers this
nods appreciatively.
Because they tell a story
she says.

Exactly.

Mr. Tanaka needs two students

to go to the library
pick up the bin of books
Ms. Cleary the librarian
put together for our class study
of France.
He sends me
and Olivia.

We walk down the hall

together   but not
Olivia   and me

until the doorway to the library
forces us

closer   together

almost touching.

Olivia steps back
lets me go in first
alone.

We each take hold
of one side of the bin
carry it between us
down the hallway
toward our class

—books
between us

stories
linking us
like Iris and the bookshop man
only I couldn't stand it
if Olivia and I ended
the same way
never seeing one another
after this chapter
is over.

My feet stop moving
just before we arrive
at our classroom.
Olivia has to stop too
looks at me
questioning.
I hold my bin handle with one hand
sign with the other:

> **I'm sorry**
> **for what I did**

sorry
for what I said.
I don't hate you
could never hate you.
I'm sorry.

Olivia drops her gaze
stares at the floor tiles
not answering
refusing
to look at me.
Then her head jerks up
and she makes a face that says
yikes!
tells me Mr. Tanaka just called out
asked if we were planning to stay out here
all day
said they were all waiting
and I think he means
they're waiting
for us to be friends again
but really
they just need the books
about France.

Olivia steps toward the door
tugs the bin along
tugging me
but I stand firm.

>   Remember going to the library together
>   at the beginning
>   of second grade?
>   Mr. Tanaka came in
>   with his sixth-graders
>   so big
>   so old
>   and we pretended
>   we weren't even scared of them
>   but we were?

Olivia laughs
maybe forgetting for a moment
that she's mad.

>   *I was scared*
she says.
>   You were all *We're just as cool*
>   *as they are.*

>   And now we're the sixth-graders
I say.
>   I wonder if the little kids
>   are afraid of *us.*

She glances toward the class
smile fading.
>   We should go in.

I try once more:
>   I miss you.

**You're supposed to be
part of my story.**

Olivia's brow scrunches.
I circle my fist on my chest
once more.
    I'm sorry.

Slowly—so slowly
it feels like waiting for a sunflower
to turn toward light
—she turns her head
toward me.

    Okay
she says.
    **I'm sorry too
    for saying that thing
    about your dad.**
She pauses.
Grimaces.
    **And for ignoring you
    in Art.**

The book bin suddenly seems lighter
the hallway brighter.

    **Want to come over after school
    to work on our projects?**
she asks

and I know
she's missed me too.

I want to go—really want to—
but I think of Iris
waiting to visit Marjorie.

     Or
I say
     **we could go
     on a field trip.**

It's only a couple of blocks
—four stops
along the bus route—
but these days it's too far
for Iris to walk.

Iris and Olivia and I climb off the bus
in front of a low building
with a long row
of windows.
We file along a petunia-lined walkway
pull open the double doors
step inside
where an odd mix of smells
greets us:
the sharp scent of cleanser
layered with a softer
rich
homey smell
...banana bread?

I look across the lounge area on my left
where a few people relax on couches
two men in wheelchairs
work a puzzle at the table

and I spy the source
of the good part of the smell.
A kitchen area
where two women who must be near Iris's age
are clapping
while a younger man
lifts a loaf pan above his head
like an athlete
hoisting a trophy.

A nurse stands behind the reception desk.
When she spots Iris
she lights up
bright as the Tweety Birds
flitting across her scrub top.
She comes around the desk
hugs Iris
shakes hands
with Olivia and me
then disappears down a long hallway.
A couple minutes later
she's back
pushing an old woman
in a wheelchair.

Iris grins
like a kid at the entrance
to Disneyland
and I know
this must be Marjorie.

The nurse—Natalee—
parks Marjorie in her wheelchair
next to a table.

"Girls," says Iris
"this is Marjorie."

Marjorie frowns
—almost a scowl.
She looks us over
speaks to Iris.
Olivia interprets
as much as she can.

>   **I don't know you.**

>   **I'm Iris. We've been friends
>   a long time.**

>   **Who are these kids?**

>   **New friends of mine—they came
>   to meet you.**

>   **Why?**

To hear your stories.

As it turns out
Marjorie doesn't seem to have the words
to tell her stories.
Not today.
Iris fills in the blanks.

"She was a pilot, you know"
Iris says
face turned to me
so I can see her words.

A pilot?

At the moment
I can't imagine Marjorie
steering her wheelchair
never mind sitting at the controls
flying a plane.
I must've misunderstood.

    A what?
I ask.

Iris carefully forms the letters

    p-i-l-o-t

and my mouth drops open
in surprise.

Really?
I say.
Iris nods
begins telling us more.
I look to Olivia
for help
hope she won't mind
interpreting.

> **She flew a courier plane**
> **did some charter work**
> **for a few years**
> **at a time when there weren't many women**
> **in the job.**

> **How did you two meet?**
I ask.
> **You weren't...**

I imagine a rainbow goddess
orange flight uniform
zipping around real rainbows
in a jet.

But no.
Iris says they met
at the airport
but she never wanted to fly planes
herself.

Movement catches my eye.
One of the older women
in the kitchen
is doing some kind of dance
gesturing
with oven mitts on her hands.

I turn my gaze back
to scowling Marjorie
wonder how she and Iris
ever became friends
so different, it seems.
But maybe they weren't always
so different.
What other stories are hiding
behind that scowl?

Later
as we wait for the bus
that will carry us home
Iris starts talking.
Olivia interprets again.

**That's where I'm going.
Rosewood Manor—or as I like to call it
The Home for People Whose Stories
are Ending.
Not the same unit
as Marjorie
but that building.**

Just one room
no kitchen to myself
someone else cooking my meals
setting my schedule.

The people seem nice
I say
thinking of Natalee's bright face.
Iris doesn't comment.

After a moment
she begins speaking again
and Olivia signs for me.

It breaks my heart
every time I see her.
No one imagines this
—no one plans
to lose their memories
their independence
the ability
to tell their story.

We'll have to tell it for her
Olivia says
and she's right.
People need to know
Marjorie is more than a scowl
more than a lady in a wheelchair
more than someone who's losing
her words.

And what about Iris?
What about her stories?

As the bus bumps along
turns onto Pemberton Street
sends Olivia crashing
into my shoulder
I'm thinking
of my school project
—family stories
that I don't really
want to tell
but someday might

(possibly
but not likely)

be glad
I did.

The first leaves

are easy.
Pale green construction paper
pencil outline
carefully cut
into a leaf shape.

I start with Mom
write

                    Rachel McMillan

along the midline
of the leaf
then fill in the story lines
—words that tell
how Mom fits
into my family tree
how she fits
into my story.
I print them as neatly
as I can
along the vein lines
of the leaf

                    mother
                    helper
                    teammate.

I add her birthday
and mine
—the date our stories
started.

I create leaves
for my grandparents
and my uncle
and even make one
for me
because I suppose
that's where my story begins.

> *Macy McMillan*
> *October 16, 2005*
> *daughter*
> *gardener*
> *book lover.*

I gather the leaves
the first pages
of my book
and imagine the story
they tell...

Does my story
start with me?
Or does it start with my mom
or my grandmother
or...

Our stories all seem
to overlap.

For the first time
in a long while
I wonder
about my father.
Olivia was right
about me not knowing
his name.
Mom always said
he wasn't meant to be
part of our lives
and mostly
that's okay with me.
But even so
his story and mine
are linked.

I cut out another leaf
leave it blank
tuck it
on the bottom of the pile.

That's all I need
—and to be honest
that's all I want.

Iris hands me a sheet of paper
glass of lemonade
sugar & spice cookie
—*you are loved*
you belong.

I settle on a kitchen chair
to read.

*I dreamed of owning a cookie shop—baking for hours each day
listening to my customers' troubles and quietly slipping an extra cookie
into their box, chosen especially to fit what they had to say.*

*I worked and planned, found a business partner to help me
make my dream come true. She ended up taking everything I had.
I'd never suspected she made a nasty habit of dishonesty.*

*Out of money (and dreams), I took my disappointed self to the want ads
saw a listing for the airport café, took a job working
for someone chasing their own dreams. It wasn't all bad—*

I met Marjorie because of it. Way back then, she took flying
lessons every Thursday. I always gave her one of my oatmeal
cookies—you can do this!—because the world was so often saying

she couldn't. And I learned that having someone steal
my money wasn't as terrible as I'd once thought. You could say
I learned to love such unexpected twists a great deal.

If Iris can bake cookies
that give someone courage
to become a pilot
imagine what amazing things
might've happened
if she'd had a whole bakery
a cookie shop
full of magical messages
for those who needed them.

But that didn't happen
because Iris's business partner
wasn't who Iris thought she was.

How could she not know
not suspect?
Didn't she check out
this person's story
before becoming partners?

I point to the words
                    I'd never suspected...
Couldn't she tell?

Iris sets her glass on the table
flips the page
writes for a few seconds.

> *I don't know that anyone*
> *is exactly*
> *who they say they are.*

The last soccer game of the season
we lose 2–1.
Jennifer Blister scored one goal
against us
but she also scored
the one *for* us
so it all evened out.

After the game
the whole team is invited
to Jennifer's.
We pile into her house
leave a jumble of soccer boots
in the entranceway.
All the parents cluster
in the kitchen.
A bunch of the kids zip right back outside
for a turn
on the backyard trampoline
and a few of us follow Jennifer
to her room.

Three huge posters hang
on the wall—black-and-white shots
of a ballerina
in different poses.
A bulletin board
displays a collection of ribbons.
I point to the ribbons
ask what they're for.

    B-a-l-l-e-t
Jennifer fingerspells.
    I love—

She starts spelling ballet again.
I interrupt
show her the sign.
She tries again
with a grin.

    I love ballet.

Then she catches Olivia's eye
speaks to her instead.
Olivia explains:

    She says she only plays soccer
    because she likes
    being part of the team.

After Jennifer turns away
to chat
with some other girls
Olivia signs
so only I can see.
     Dance...I never would've guessed.

It's surprising
the things we don't know
about people
surprising how often their stories
aren't what we expect

which reminds me
of Marjorie.

Later, while my mom
is driving me and Olivia home
I nudge Olivia
say
     Remember when you said
     we should tell Marjorie's story
     for her?

     Yeah
says Olivia.
     Why?

     I'm wondering
     how we can do that.

Olivia purses her lips
taps her chin.
Mom pulls the car up to the curb
in front of Olivia's.
Olivia unbuckles her seatbelt
turns to face me.

I've got an idea
she says
waggling her eyebrows.
If
you're up for an adventure.

Sunday afternoon

Alan holds out a box
lid open—donuts
with pink
orange
blue
brown frosting
multicolors
looking like a sugary garden
in a flimsy white box.

**I stopped at that little bakery
on Anderson Street**
he says
signing a bit awkwardly
fingerspelling *bakery*
and *Anderson.*

I can picture that shop
—the big storefront window
wedding cakes on display
and inside
air heavy with sugar and yeast
room crowded

people queuing up
mouths watering
while they wait for their turn
to order
gawking
at the glass cabinet
full of breads
muffins
donuts
cookies.

Cookies...like Iris
might've had in her own bakery
if her dream
had come true
if people had been
who they said they were.

I look up from the bakery box
Alan's striped shirt
stubbly chin
gentle smile that just might be
hiding something.

If nobody is exactly
who they say they are
who
exactly
is Alan?

And if he's not exactly the Alan
Mom thinks he is
maybe she won't marry him
after all.

    Take your pick
he says
still extending the box
toward me.
    A little treat
    for you.

No way
am I eating one of those.

    Not hungry
I say.

Mom intervenes.
    You love Anderson's donuts.

I shrug
and turn away
just as Alan glances at Mom
with a subtle shake
of his head
and a look of frustration
like he just
can't
win.

The next bus

will pass Rosewood Manor
in a half hour.
Iris, Olivia, and I
chat with Marjorie
in the lounge
keeping an eye
on the time.

After a nod from Iris
Olivia grips the handles
of Marjorie's wheelchair
I link my arm
through Iris's
and we tell Natalee
we're taking Marjorie out
for some fresh air.
We roll right out the front door
down the sidewalk
to the bus stop.
When the bus arrives
with a wave of heat
a stench of exhaust
the driver lowers the ramp
helps Marjorie board.

We transfer buses
at Tenth and Arlington
finally arrive
at the municipal airport.
The glass doors slide open
automatically
and when we step inside
I feel
triumphant.
Olivia's idea was genius.
When we told Iris our airport scheme
we figured it would take some convincing
but Iris loved the idea
right away.

We park Marjorie in her chair
next to a giant window
that's really more of a see-through wall
and we take in the view
—planes coming and going
baggage carts zipping about
people in neon vests
waving
their arms.

Marjorie's scowl
hasn't slipped
and I can't tell if she's pleased
to be here.

But then she says
"I was a pilot, you know."
And there's a hint
a spark
a light in her eyes
I never noticed
before.

It's that spark
that makes me believe
she's one of Iris's Firecracker friends.

When we return to Rosewood Manor
Natalee doesn't greet us
with her usual enthusiasm.
Instead, we get hands on hips
stern face
telling us
we're in big trouble.

Olivia takes charge
steps forward
chin lifted
signing as she presents
our excuse.

We were telling Marjorie a story.
I suppose
we lost track of time.

Natalee comes around
relieves me of wheelchair duty
peers at us
skeptically.

As we turn to leave
Iris is wearing a small
but unmistakeably satisfied
smile.

I enlist Olivia to help me
because she's the best researcher
I know

(not counting Ms. Cleary
the school librarian
who can find out everything
about anything).

Finding information
gossip
facts for school reports
is Olivia's specialty.
I tell her I need info about Alan
for my family history project
—not the truest thing
I might've said—
and something inside me
suddenly feels a bit off
like a bad taste lingering
in my mouth.
I swallow it down.

Why don't you just ask him?
Olivia says.

**He's too busy
with wedding stuff.**

I think my mom
is doing most of the wedding stuff
but it sounds
like a believable excuse.
But then just like that
the bad taste
is back.

Who knew a person
could taste lies?

(Turns out
they're a bit like pineapple
after it's been sitting too long
in the fridge
stewing
in its own juice.)

Olivia is my best friend.

Am I a person who lies
to her best friend?

Actually
I tell her
it's not for the project.

She grins
a mischievous kind of grin
that says she loves the idea
of spying
sneaking
getting the dirt
on my stepdad-to-be.
It doesn't feel quite so good
to me
but what choice
do I have?
It's the only way
to stop the wedding.

Olivia and I gobble our lunches
dash to the library
pull two chairs close
and log on
to one of the computers.
This morning I asked Mom
where Alan was born
what his full name is
and let her think I needed the facts
for my project.
Now, Olivia types his name
in the search box.

Ms. Cleary wanders toward us.
I elbow Olivia
and she glances up
clicking over to the library's homepage
just as Ms. Cleary
stops
at our desk.

Need any help?
she asks
and we both shake our heads
say no
a little too quickly.
Ms. Cleary's smile disappears.
She says something
I don't catch
but when she comes around behind us
to glance at the monitor
I know
she's suspicious.

Olivia starts talking
signs for my benefit
babbles about how you never really know
the true stories about people's past.
Why did she say
all that?

She looks super-guilty
even though digging for the truth
is maybe not
such a terrible thing
to do.

Ms. Cleary's eyebrows
knit together
so I jump in
start signing
tell her about Marjorie.

She shakes her head
says
I don't understand.

I start again
and Olivia interprets for Ms. Cleary
tries to keep up
signals me to
s l o w   d o w n.

I sigh
then try one more time
to tell her about Marjorie
the pilot
how you'd never guess it
to look at her now
—but why not?

Why do we think
we can know anything about a person
by how they look
what they can do
what life is like for them now?
Because it turns out
we really can't.
The only way to know that stuff
is if someone
tells you the story.

Whew.

I blab even more
than Olivia.

Olivia takes a minute
to catch up with my words
does the best she can
gives up when my hands
get going too quickly again
but even so
Ms. Cleary's eyebrows
finally relax.
She walks away
disappears into the stacks
comes back a few minutes later

with a smile and a book
about women
in aviation.

She hands the book to me
says
**Maybe your friend
is in here.**
Then she shrugs
says, "You never know."

You never do.

Which reminds me of my mission
which is about Alan
not Marjorie
or airplanes
or history
but
I'm definitely checking out this book
for later.

Ms. Cleary goes back to her desk
and Olivia
goes back to searching.

By the time lunch break ends
we haven't found anything
except where Alan works
as a dentist
—which is no secret—
but Olivia jots notes
on a scrap of paper
stuffs it in her jeans pocket
vows to search until she uncovers
something juicy.

Mom flicks through dresses

on the rack
not really looking
just passing the time
while we wait.
The shopkeeper emerges
from the back
our dresses slung
over her arm.
The woman shoos us
into change rooms.
I try on the lavender dress
freshly hemmed
decide to ask Mom
for new sandals
to go with it.

Mom peeks in
says
    Beautiful
then beckons me.
    Come and see.

I slide the curtain aside
step out
where Mom poses
in her wedding dress.
Vintage, she calls it
not quite white
antique lace
knee length.
No veil
no trailing skirt
but it's exactly right
for her.

Back at home
we climb out of the car
collect our dresses
shoes
the pale lipstick
Mom said I could wear
for the wedding
and it's only then
—walking up to the house
I'll be leaving—
that the day's shine
falls away
a cloud
moving over the sun
as I remember
what it's all leading up to.

Iris stands on her front step
swishes a broom
one way
then the other.
She pauses
waves
chats with Mom
for a minute.

    She wants to brighten up
    the front of her house
Mom tells me
    so it appeals
    to buyers. She wants to know
    if it's too late
    to plant nasturtiums.

    It's fine
I say.
    They grow fast.
    Tell her I can plant them for her
    if she'd like.

Iris would like that
very much
so after I stow my wedding outfit
in my room
I go next door.

Iris pulls an envelope of seeds
from her apron pocket
points out a large pot
and I get to work
loosen the soil
press round seeds
into dark earth
shower them with water.

Now we wait
I say
both hands palm up
wiggling my fingers.

Iris extends the leaf-green notebook.

You're a good neighbor, Macy.
I'll miss you.

My eyes sting
as if it's a big deal
Iris is moving one place
and I'm moving another.

But that's crazy...

except that
it's not.

I ask for the pen
write below her message.

You're coming to the wedding
aren't you?

I wouldn't miss it
for anything.

As I cross the lawn
to my house
I glance back at the pot
flower seeds waiting
to sprout
and I know
I'll be long gone
before they do.

Construction paper
scissors
marker.

Iris Gillan
neighbor
rainbow goddess
storyteller
friend.

I add the leaf
to my project.

A message from Olivia
pops up
on the computer.

Jackpot!

My heart speeds up
thuds madly
beneath my ribs.

She found something?
Something big?

I glance over my shoulder.
Mom's curled up
on the corner of the couch
lost in a book

but then
argh!

she looks up at me
smiles
says

**It must be time
for bed.**

I message Olivia back.

Can't chat now.

But I have to know
so I add

Mission accomplished?

Her reply appears
a moment later.

Definitely.

Wow.
I knew it.
This is awesome.

I log off
say goodnight to Mom
go upstairs
but there's no way
I'll be able to sleep.

It's ages before I drift off
then I sleep late
wonder why the vibrations from my alarm
didn't wake me
until I realize
I forgot to set it.
I miss walking to school with Olivia
dash into class late
and earn a recess detention
from Mr. Tanaka.
Finally at lunch
Olivia and I get a chance to talk
in private.
She's near breathless
with the news.

You won't believe it
she says.
I found a newspaper article.
It's crazy.

Tell me!

The twins
—he kidnapped them!

Kidnapped?

Four years ago.
He took them
to M-e-x-i-c-o.

No.
I can't think
can't believe.
This makes
no
sense.

> **You mean**
> **they're not his kids?**

Olivia's eyes are saucers
as she tells me the details.

> **They are.**
> **He was married before, right?**
> **He took the girls**
> **and his wife reported it**
> **sent the police after him**
> **hauled them back**
> **over the border.**
> **No wonder she divorced him!**

The twins would've been
two years old
and he...

whoa.

This is big.

This is enormous.

This
is miles better
than I'd hoped

—and miles
worse.

After school

we rush to my room
close the door.
Olivia pulls a folded paper
from her back pocket
opens it to reveal
a news article
she printed from the Internet.
Her hands
smooth the creases
slide the page
toward me
finger tapping at the headline.

Local Dentist Questioned in Kidnapping Case

I scan the article
see his name
twin girls
taken
Mexico
but it feels like I'm reading
about strangers.

**Is this a real newspaper
or a gossip one?**
I ask Olivia.

**It's real.
I'm pretty sure.
It'll do the trick
and you won't have to move
to the new house.
It'll stay just you
and your mom.**

I should be excited
and part of me is
but there's a seed
of sadness
buried deep inside
that I'm trying to pretend
isn't there.

**It's what you wanted
right?**
says Olivia.

I refold the page
tuck it behind the books
on my shelf.

Olivia and I head to the dining room
where it appears as if a craft store
exploded.
I guess I should've cleaned up
after my last failed attempt
at crafting.

We twist
shape
tie
until the last of the centerpieces
is complete.
All that work
—that not-my-specialty work—
finally finished
thanks to Olivia.
I'd be sunk
if she weren't part
of my story.

That night before bed
I cut another leaf
pale green construction paper
write her name
her birthday
and the date we met
—first day
of second grade—
add details of our story
words like veins
in the leaf

best friend
expert crafter.

I need more
another story line
but for now
this is perfect.

We're barely in the door

twins swarm me
shepherding me
toward the stairs
both of them trying
to sign something
without a pause
in their perpetual motion.

Room. They're signing *room*
—even Kaitlin, now that her finger
is fixed. They pull me
into Alan's barren box of an office.
It's utterly empty
utterly drab.

Alan the kidnapper appears
at my shoulder.

> **It's ready any time**
> **you want to move stuff in**

he says.

> **You mean never?**

His face falls.
Mom rebukes
but she doesn't know the truth.
Why is it so hard
to tell her?
To blurt it out?

Maybe if the twins
weren't right here.
As pesky as they are
they're not to blame
for their dad
being a kidnapper.
Mom's not to blame either
but she needs to know.

I focus on the beige wall.
Can I paint it?

Judging by the rest
of his bland house
he'll say no
to color
which might as well be no
to joy
—one more reason
he's not stepdad material.
But the kidnapper says
What color?

Purple
—not lavender
or lilac
but bright
bold
lupine purple.

I'm sure that crosses the line
is more than Bland Kidnapper Man
can take.

"Purple?" he says.
He turns to the twins
signs as he speaks to them.
She wants a purple room!

Bethany and Kaitlin
eyes round
mouths dropping open
suddenly bounce across the hallway
like jumping beans.

Kaitlin flings open their door
and I peer in
—bunk beds with polka-dot quilts
fuschia rug
bold purple walls.

I can't help it
—a smile
sneaks onto my face.

Mom taps my shoulder.
    Alan has something to show you
    outside.

I follow her
the twins follow me
a ragtag parade
through the house
out
to the backyard.

I jerk to a stop
wide-eyed.

Almost half
of the not-very-big-to-begin-with lawn
is torn up
gone
leaving a plot
of freshly turned earth
rich
and dark.

    For you
Alan says
    if you want.
    Plant whatever you like
    maybe dig up a few things
    from your old house
    to get you started.

I gawk at the garden plot
turn to stare
at Alan.
Bethany is hanging
off one side of him
Kaitlin
the other side
all three of them
grinning.

Thank you
I say
too stunned
to say anything more.

Maybe I won't tell Mom
just yet.
Maybe she doesn't have to know
about the kidnapping
today...

but the days
are running out.

Uncle Caleb's plane arrives late
on Friday afternoon.
We have to dash
from the airport to the church
so we're not late
for the rehearsal.
Gran and Grampa got into town yesterday.
Gran had barely settled in
before she started cooking up a storm
preparing for tonight's special dinner
filling the house
with mouth-watering smells
—cabbage rolls
roast beef
chocolate cake.

We park beside the church
rush inside.
Everyone else
is already here
—Alan's mother
brother
brother's wife
Mom's friends Macy and Duckie
—all here
for a practice run

so we'll know where to stand
what to do
for the wedding.
There's an interpreter—James—
who will sign
the whole wedding service.
Now, Mom and Alan face each other
as the minister explains
about the vows
and suddenly it feels
so real.
How did I let it get this far?
It's really happening.

It can't.

Mom and I are a perfect team
a just-right-as-we-are story
and I can't stand
losing that.

The little seed of sadness
or guilt
that's been nagging me
since I asked Olivia to help me research
tries to push through.
I bury it
a bit deeper.
I'm almost out of time
must stop this
tonight.

When the rehearsal's over
we pile into cars
drive back to the house
pour into the living room and overflow
to the kitchen.
Gran pulls cabbage rolls from the oven
a layered salad from the fridge
while Uncle Caleb pours drinks.

Duckie slips me a glass
of champagne
—pale gold
and fizzy
like ginger ale.
I take a sip
sputter
cough
leave the glass by a lamp
on the end table.

Bethany and Kaitlin climb
into Mom's rocking chair
get it zipping
back
     and forth
so fast
     I'm sure
they'll tip
     but they
don't.

All around the room
jaws flap
as everyone yakety-yaks
laughing
joking
nobody bothering
to sign.
I sure could use James now
but I won't see him again
until tomorrow
at the church.
The crowd seems to close in.
This is happening
—all of it—
the wedding
the move
the wrecking of my family
and life
as I know it.
I need to escape
to my garden
or curl up
in the window seat
disappear in a book
but I'm trapped
in my own house
lost
in my own story.

Wait.

Am I writing this story?

Movement around me stops
like someone hit the pause button
faces all turn
toward the kitchen doorway
where my mom stands
glowing.

"Dinner's ready,"
she says.

We can't all fit
around the table.
People fill their plates
with Gran's cooking
claim seats
wherever they can find one
sit with their dinner
on their lap.

      Aren't you going to eat?
Mom asks me.

      I can't
I tell her.
      I feel sick.

She's never done the typical mom-thing
the hand-on-forehead thing
but of course
I don't have a fever
anyway.
Instead
Mom tips her head
to one side
purses her lips
tries to see
inside my thoughts.

I cross my arms
over my chest
set my jaw.
Mom's brows
scrunch together.

It's now
or never.

A little paint
and a garden plot
don't erase that news story
—I *know* what I saw
what I read
what he did.

I take a big breath
let it out
and then my hands
take over.

      You can't marry him
I say.
      You can't.
      You don't know
      because he seems nice
      acts nice
      but really
      he's a horrible person.
      You need
      to call the wedding
      off.

Mom's face changes

from confused
to angry
with a large dash
of embarrassed.
Her eyes flash at me
cheeks flaming.

    That's quite enough
she says.

The room is still
all eyes searching
from me
to Mom
questioning
unsure
what we're saying.

I block them out
turn back
to Mom.

    You need to know this
I say.
    He took them.

I gesture
toward the twins.
> **Kidnapped them**
> **disappeared**
> **to Mexico.**
> **What kind of father**
> **does that?**

> **That's ridiculous.**

She doesn't believe me
must believe me.
Is it even safe
for us to be with him?
Mom turns away
speaks to her friends
family
the kidnapper
all gathered
squeezed into our kitchen.
By habit
her hands move
as she speaks.

> **I'm so sorry.**
> **I don't know**
> **what's gotten into Macy.**

No. It's not me.
It's him.

She needs to know
needs to believe me
she can't marry him.

I slam my fist
on the table
silverware jumps
attention snaps
to me.
Anger and fear
rush through me
arm flings out
finger stabs
at Alan
and a single word
bursts
from my mouth.

"Kidnapper!"

No one moves.
Uncle Caleb is frozen
a slab of roast
skewered on his fork
suspended halfway
between the platter
and his plate.

Then the kidnapper stands
gestures helplessly at Mom

mouth moving
in what must be
a nasty lie
or a lousy excuse.

I bang the table again.
Alan's gaze flicks to me.

Sign!

He signs carefully
deliberately.

It wasn't like that.

Mom gapes at him.
But it happened?

Sort of. Not really.

Mom reaches for a chair
face lily white
sinks
onto the seat.

Alan steps toward me
like he wants to keep this private
just between us
but it's too late
way too late.

    You've got it wrong
he says.
    You don't understand.

I move back.
    I understand.
    You're a kidnapper
    can't be trusted
    and there's no way
    you
    are going to be
    my stepdad.

I push my way out of the room
past Duckie
wild friend Macy
Grampa
glance back
and see Alan and his brother
heads bent
talking
probably plotting.
Maybe they're both
kidnappers
a whole family
of kidnappers.
I search out Bethany and Kaitlin.
Should I take them with me
rescue them
protect them?

I turn away
stride down the hall
close myself
in my room.

Alone

away from the crowd
and the kidnapper
I curl up on my bed
face the wall
swipe at my cheeks.
For some stupid reason
I'm crying
can't stop
no matter how hard
I squeeze shut my eyes.

I had to do it.

And now
the wedding's off.
Of course
the wedding will be off.
My mom would never
marry a kidnapper
on purpose.

After forever
I turn over
pull up the neck of my tee shirt
to dry my face.
Now would be a good time
to be in my garden
satiny petals
tickly leaves
array of colors
perfect blend
of sharp and soothing scents
all working together
to cheer me up.

I'm not sure
why I need cheering up.

When my door beacon flashes
I know it's Mom
wanting to come in
and I'm so ready
for a hug.

I open the door
but there's no hug
no open arms
and definitely
no cheering up.

Mom steps inside
shoves the door closed
sits me down
and starts to lecture.
The fire in her eyes
shoots out through her hands
punctuates
her signs.

      How could you?
Mom says.
      If you really thought
      he was a kidnapper
      you should've asked me about it
      in private
      talked to me sooner
      —not wait until now
      not blurt it out
      in front of everyone
      not ruin
      this special night.

Why is she so angry
at me?
She's supposed to be mad
at Alan.

      But he *is* a kidnapper!
      I wanted to tell you before
      but I couldn't.

Mom looks up at the ceiling
as if searching
for calm
takes a slow breath
turns her attention
back to me.
    Alan is most definitely
    not
    a kidnapper.

    But the newspaper said—

    Stop
she says
bringing one hand down
slapping the side of it
against her other palm.
    You need to hear
    Alan's side of the story.

She sits on my bed
tucks one leg up
reaches
for my hands.
I wait
letting her hold my hands.
She finally releases them
smoothes my hair
sighs.

Then she tells me
the whole thing.

Afterward
Mom leaves me in my room
tells me to stay there
not return
to the party.

I'm banished.

I sneak into Mom's office
log on
to her computer
email Olivia and tell her
how Alan's ex-wife Alexis
had problems
wasn't stable...
how the trip to Mexico
was meant to be a family vacation
the first time
they'd been on holiday
since the twins were born
planning
tickets
excitement
but then Alexis
couldn't deal with it
decided she couldn't go
wouldn't go
needed time alone
to think
and rest.

I tell her how Alan and the girls
went without Alexis
and then she changed her mind
wanted them back
but instead of just missing them
she got angry
made accusations
called the police and said Alan
took the kids
ran off
left the country.

And finally I tell Olivia how
after they came home
got things straightened out
police left
dust settled
Alexis told Alan
she wanted a divorce
didn't want to be married
anymore
and in the end
she didn't want the girls
either.

Olivia messages me back
a single word:

Oops.

A minute later
another email appears
an apology
and I can tell Olivia feels awful
but really
it's my fault.

I log off
slip back down the hall
to my room
flop
onto the bed.

I haven't put a stop
to the wedding
to Alan
becoming my stepfather
to leaving my garden
my window seat for reading
my red front door
on Pemberton Street.
All I've done
is make everyone
mad at me.

I believe
I'm in the depths
of despair.

The strange thing
is that seed of sadness
and guilt
—the one I buried deep
so it wouldn't stop me
from digging for dirt
on Alan—
that seed
seems
to be sprouting
unfurling
and it's not at all
what I expected.

My family history project
—such as it is—
lies in a heap on my desk
a pile of paper leaves
raked up
not looking much like a project
at all
more like a mess.
I pick up the pile
straighten the leaves
so they all line up
flip through them
one
after
another.

My thoughts drift
to the dining room
Mom's anger
Alan's hurt.
Drift farther
to the new room
purple walls
girls happily clinging
to Alan.
Drift outside
to a garden plot
fresh earth
turned
for me.
I see Alan signing
remember when he and Mom met
he didn't know any signs at all.
And I think
if he can try
to understand my story
maybe
possibly
I can try
to understand his.

That seed
that perhaps was telling me
not to do it
not to go after Alan
not to wreck Mom's wedding
was actually telling me

Alan
is okay
and he might even turn out to be
a good stepdad.

Maybe even
a good
dad.

It'll be nice to know
my dad's name.

My gaze falls
to the paper leaves
in my hands.
I set the pile aside
reach for three sheets
of green construction paper
trace outlines
cut new leaves.
With a black marker
I write Alan's name and birthdate
on the first one.
I add tomorrow's date
—the wedding—
fill in story threads
along the vein lines

stepfather
garden digger
not a kidnapper

On the other new leaves
I write Bethany's name
Kaitlin's name
realize I don't know
their birthday
don't know really
how they fit into my story
except for one thing.
I write carefully on each one
with purple marker:

Sister

Saturday comes

like I knew it would
sure as the sunrise
on a summer day.
The sky is forget-me-not blue.
It looks like a perfect day
for a perfect wedding
except that everything
is going wrong.

I'm not as sad about that
as I should be
because the truth is
I can whip through chapter after chapter
of a good book
but starting a new chapter
of my own story
is not
my specialty.

Mom slept in
missed her hair appointment
because she lay awake for hours
worrying

and probably stewing
about me
what I said last night.
She pins her hair up
takes it down
tries again
glances at the clock
and frowns.

> **The florist should've been here
> by now.**

She's finally happy
with her hair
looks again at the time
phones the florist
her face reddening
as she listens, talks, listens some more.
By the time she hangs up, tears
are running down her face.

> **They messed up.**

she tells me.

> **They've got no record of my order
> even though I checked
> and double-checked.**

> **What does that mean?**

> **No bouquets for us girls
> no boutonniere for Alan.**

**They said they could put something together
quickly
from whatever they have
but it won't be
what I ordered.**

Does it have to be?

I wanted white roses.

I know, but—

**I yelled at the poor florist
said I didn't want a bouquet
of leftovers.**

Mom sinks onto the couch
face in her hands
shoulders shaking.
I put a hand on her back
wait
unsure
what to do.

I stare out the living-room window
clear blue sky
marred only
by the long white trail
of a jet.

Marjorie.

All these things going wrong
might seem like signs
bits of story
that don't belong
that say we're going
the wrong way.
But if we listen to those things
to setbacks and disappointments
if we let fear or worry
stop us from trying
from turning the page
we'll never get to meet
the Marjories of life
never find out
how great our story
could be.

Mom and Alan first met
at the supermarket
when Alan bashed Mom's ankle
with his shopping cart.
Forgetting to be mom-like
she swore
then saw the twins
apologized
got chatting with Alan.
She never planned
on meeting someone at the store
never planned
on getting her ankle slammed

but now
they're getting married
their stories coming together
like a plot twist.

Mom wipes her eyes
smudging
her mascara.

    It doesn't matter
I tell her.
    The hairdresser, the florist.
    What matters
    is that you and Alan
    are getting married.

A feeble smile
pulls at her mouth.
    You're right
she says.
    I don't even care
    about the flowers.

It looks like she cares
more than she'll admit.
She goes to put on her dress

and I slip outside
to my garden
gather a handful
of long stems
—daisies, larkspur, mallow—
take a long bit of lavender ribbon
left over from the centerpieces
wrap it
around the stems
tie a bow
and leave the ends
trailing.

It's not exactly white roses
but when I hand it to Mom
stress falls away
joy blooms
on her face
and I know
I've done something right.

Alan and the twins

stand at the front of the church
Alan shiny clean
beaming
as he looks past me in the aisle
to Mom, behind me
with her not-long dress
not-fancy hairstyle
not-white-roses bouquet.
I feel a little invisible
until I see Bethany and Kaitlin
in their lavender dresses
bouncing on their toes
grinning madly
hands flapping in my direction
in a too-excited wave.

I take my place at the front
turn a little
to watch Mom approach.
She looks beautiful.
Radiant.
Extravagantly
happy.

I don't know why
I have to look away.
I scan the church
my gaze flitting across pews.
Gran, Grampa, and Uncle Caleb
Macy and Duckie
Desi's mom, from sign language group
Alan's family
and strangers who must be friends
of my family-to-be.

I look again
more carefully
stomach knotting.

Mom reaches the front of the church
Alan takes her hand
they face the minister
but I catch Mom's attention
sign to her
worried now
because late
is not something I'd expect
from Iris.

Mom glances out at the people
gathered in pews.
I look too.

Iris is definitely not here.
Iris
is missing.

    Maybe she just wasn't up to it
Mom says.
    Don't worry.

    No
I sign back.
    She said she'd be here.
    Something's wrong.
    I have to check on her
    have to find her.

    But it's time—

    I have to find her!

I don't wait for her to respond
move from my place
hurry down the aisle
ignoring the puzzled looks
on people's faces.
I pull open the big door
sun streaming in
don't look back
and run.

Turns out, it's hard to run
in a lavender dress
and sandals with heels.
I stop to pull off my shoes
and Alan catches up to me.

Wait
he says.
I'll help you look.

He gets his car
and we drive to Pemberton Street
not far at all
but we don't see Iris
along the way.
I push the button for her doorbell
bang on the door
try the handle—locked.

Back in Alan's car
drive to the end of Pemberton
turn right
turn again
drive down the next street
and the next
my heart thudding
in my chest.
Something's wrong
I know it.

What if she's actually in her house
but couldn't make it
to the door?
What if she needs an ambulance
again?

Her story can't end
like that.

It just can't.

Another corner
another empty street.

We've covered
almost the whole neighborhood.
Alan glances at the clock
on the dash.
He wants to go back
get married
forget
about Iris.

We have to keep looking!

He nods
turns down the next road.

Someone is up ahead
on the sidewalk
—and that someone
is wearing an orange skirt
floral blouse
comfortable shoes
dragging an oxygen tank behind her
in a little cart.

I let out a breath.

Alan pulls up alongside Iris
and I hop out.
Iris turns
and the enormous Tupperware container
under her arm
threatens to tumble
to the ground.
I lurch forward
catch it
before it falls.

"Did I miss it?" Iris asks.
"I got lost." She lets go of the handle
for the oxygen cart
fingerspells
  l-o-s-t
signs
  sorry

and my heart
nearly bursts.

It's okay
I tell her.
You didn't miss it. It's okay.

Alan helps her into the car
settles the oxygen tank beside her
holds the Tupperware container
while I buckle up
and we all head back
to the church.

We gather at the front of the church again
Mom clutching
her slightly wilted wildflower bouquet
twins wiggling
Alan beaming
and Iris
sitting back-straight in the pew
beside Gran.

James interprets as Mom and Alan
say their vows
and the minister prays
blesses them
and all of us
—our newly formed family—
and then there's the kiss
and it's all official
all
so
real.

Wow.

There's a streak
of lavender
a flash
of ponytails
as Bethany and Kaitlin mob me
fling their arms around me
in a giant
bouncy
hug.
When Kaitlin lets go
she looks me in the eye
raises her closed hand
to the side of her face
slides it down to her chin
then brings her index fingers
together

Sister.

A tight lump forms
in my throat.
I repeat the sign
blink
look away
catch a glimpse of orange
—Iris.

She's standing now
enormous Tupperware container open
holding it out
to the family behind her
offering cookies to friends
and strangers
right there in the church.
When Uncle Caleb catches my eye
he grins
holds up a large brown sugar-sprinkled cookie
and takes a bite.

Sugar & spice cookies.

I can almost hear them whispering
—*You are loved*
you belong.

Mr. Tanaka collects our projects

—posters
scrapbooks
fancy family tree charts complete
with photos.
Olivia created a stand-up display
with exquisite
lettering.
Jennifer Blister hands in
a computer flash drive.

Movie
she signs
when she sees me looking.
Grandmother
Then she mimes
talking into a microphone
and I'm guessing
she made a video of her grandma
telling family stories.
Suddenly my leaf-shaped booklet
looks lame
like something I might've made
in second grade.

But the truth is
these leaves
these pages—me and my mom
my grandparents
Uncle Caleb
Olivia and Iris
Alan
and the twins
—even the blank one—
these pages tell the story
of my family
and that
was the whole point.
Maybe Mr. Tanaka will like it
and maybe he won't
but it's me
telling myself the story
of my family.

It's a story
I needed to tell.

Mr. Tanaka perches on the edge
of his desk
begins talking to the class
so I turn my attention
to Ms. Eklund.
Ms. Eklund's been my interpreter
for three years.
Now we're both done
at Hamilton Elementary.

Next year I'll be at Lloyd Edison Middle School
with a new interpreter
and Ms. Eklund is transferring
to another elementary
to work with a third-grader.

My breath catches.

I wish I'd made a leaf
for Ms. Eklund.

      You can bring snacks to share
she says.

For a moment
I'm lost
—snacks?

      The party will start
      after you've finished cleaning out
      your desks.

Oh.
The year-end party
which I should be excited about
but honestly
my feelings
are a tangled mess.

I'm halfway living at the new house
wavering
between an end
and a beginning
—some of my things are there
some are still at my Pemberton Street home.
The school year finishing
means even more change.
It means no more walking with Olivia
every morning
no more zipping over to her house
for no particular reason
at all.

I don't want to think about it.

> **Can you believe**
> **we're going to be in middle school?**

says Olivia.

> **I just know**
> **it'll be magnificent.**

Olivia's always been very good
at enthusiasm.

> **I'm planning to re-invent myself**

she says.

> **Pink hair, maybe.**
> **Start seventh grade fresh**
> **—a whole new me.**

I like the old you
I tell her.

She ignores my comment
slings an arm
over my shoulder
gives me a quick
sideways hug.

We'll have so many adventures
she says.

It's true—if there are adventures
to be had
Olivia will find them.

An image of Olivia's leaf page
leaps
into my brain
—the blank space
on her story lines.
I never finished
filling it in!

The instant we're dismissed
I dash to the front
paw through the projects
on Mr. Tanaka's desk
searching
for mine.

There!

I grab my leaf book
flip to Olivia's page
—her name
birthdate
the day we met
and our story lines written
along the leaf veins

best friend
expert crafter

_____.

I pop the lid
off a marker
fill in the final story line

firecracker.

Iris moved out

a week after the wedding
all her furniture and kitchen things
donated
to a family in need
—except her floral recliner
which moved with her
to Rosewood Manor.

We'd finished sorting her books
the day before.
She had four KEEP boxes
including one stuffed full
with journals
photos
knickknacks—including
the hip-wiggling hula dancer.
Turns out
there are as many stories
in the bits and bobs
as there are in the books

but those ones...those are the kind of stories
that need to be shared
while drinking lemonade
and eating sugar & spice cookies

baked
by a rainbow goddess

the kind of stories that start from a seed
a scrap
a spark of memory
and then
when you begin to tell them
they burst into bloom
like a field of wildflowers
on the first hot day
of summer.

No wonder Iris doesn't want
to lose them.
No wonder she hangs on
to books, clippings, memories.
They're stories
all of them.
Someday maybe
I'll have to tell them for her
and someday maybe
I'll have to tell them *to* her
—and I will
because stories
are worth saving
sharing
hanging on to
and giving away.

On Thursday
I ride my bike
all the way to Rosewood Manor
—or as I like to call it
The Home for People with Amazing Stories
to Tell.

I wave at Natalee
say hello to Marjorie.
She scowls.
I smile
and go in search
of Iris.

I find her in the sunroom
with a stout
gray-haired woman
and Simon, the activity coordinator
(the one who made banana bread
the very first day
I visited).

They're bending over a familiar box.
Iris glances up
beams
when she sees me.
"We're making a library"
she says

and sure enough
all Iris's KEEP books
are finding their way
into a sturdy bookcase.

Iris pads over
with her oxygen cart
hugs me
then steps back and signs
with her speckled hands.

Thank you.
Cookie.

Last time I was here
I cornered Simon
shared my idea
and he agreed
to help Iris bake cookies
whenever the need arises.

A rainbow goddess
needs to be able
to send messages.

Iris writes in her notebook
—a new dandelion yellow one—
then passes it to me.

I'm so thankful, but you know, dear one
the gods' messages can be sent even without cookies
—messages of courage, hope, laughter, support.
They must be sent—through cookies or stories
quiet deeds or mountaintop proclamations.
Hearts are waiting, worrying, hurting
—in need of a message
you can send.

Me?

My thoughts zip to the airport
the light in Marjorie's eyes
...to a garden bouquet
stress falling from my mother's face.
Maybe Marjorie's heart heard
Your story is important.
You matter.
Maybe Mom's heart heard
I love you.
I support you.
The idea feels warm
light rising up
inside me.

But then I see stones kicked
words hurled
accusations, anger, fear
and my spirit
sinks.

I jot a note
on a fresh page.

I've sent some terrible messages.

"We all have," she says.

I wish I could unsend some of mine.

"Wouldn't that be grand?" she says
reaching for the notebook.

*All we can do
is try to send many more good messages
than bad.
We must aim to be kind
and brave.*

Brave like a mouse
I say
brushing the end of my nose
with my finger
—the sign
for *mouse.*

Iris laughs.
*Yes, brave like Despereaux
like a certain redheaded girl
like a boy wizard and his friends
like a convict and a priest.*

A convict and... Huh?
Did I miss something?

"*Les Misérables,*" she says.
"You must read it someday."

There are so many stories
of extravagant kindness
extravagant bravery.
I'd like my life
to tell such a story.
I don't expect I'll come across
any princesses
or evil wizards
—although
you never know...
There's already a rainbow goddess
in my story
and I'm only eleven years old.

The trunk and back seat of Mom's car

are full
with the last of our belongings
from the old house.
Even the front is full
—odds and ends tucked at my feet
my "pack-last" box balancing
on my lap
carrying the books I'm reading
my toothbrush
random things I needed
or missed packing earlier.

We park in the driveway.
Alan comes outside
helps Mom unpack the car
lugging stuff inside.
Finally I climb out
trudge up the walkway
stare at the not-red front door
before pushing it open.

A flash of movement
as one of the twins darts past
and the other
streaks after her.

I close the door with my foot
take a deep breath...
and smell something delicious.
Peanut butter cookies?
But Mom doesn't bake
and besides
we just got here.
I sniff the air
set down my box
follow my nose to the kitchen.
A pan of cookies
cools on the stove
more on the counter
already on a plate.

Alan bakes?

He appears beside me.

Help yourself
he says
nodding toward the plate.
They're peanut butter.

I munch a cookie
while Alan readies another pan
for the oven.
Peanut butter cookies
—*joy, laughter.*

I hope that's a promise.
I hope I really do have good things
to look forward to here.

Up in my lupine-purple room
I begin putting stuff away
trying to make it feel
like my own space.

Light flashes
from my door beacon
—someone's knocking.
I pull open the door
still holding a stack of books
under my arm.

Bethany and Kaitlin stand side by side
antsy
but relatively still.
They look at one another
nod
then sign together

Welcome home.

Then they dash off
grinning.

Welcome home...

This is home now
truly
and it surprises me
to feel this way.

Sometimes life goes in directions
you don't expect.
Sometimes you change in ways
you never imagined.
It's hard
especially if starting new chapters
isn't your specialty.
I never dreamed
I'd end up here
—in a new house
with a dad named Alan
two little sisters
and a mom
who seems extravagantly happy.

An idea flutters within me
takes a moment
to sink
into my soul
like a butterfly landing
on a blossom
shaking out its wings
before folding them
to rest.

Maybe finding home
is about following
your story.

Once upon a time
I moved
into a lupine-purple room...

Iris Gillan's Sugar & Spice Cookies

1 cup butter
1 cup white sugar
1 cup brown sugar
2 large eggs
¼ cup molasses

3 cups flour
2 teaspoons baking soda
1 ½ teaspoon ginger
1 ½ teaspoon cinnamon
½ teaspoon salt

Preheat oven to 350°F.
Cream butter and sugars. Beat in eggs and molasses.
Combine flour, soda, and spices, in a separate bowl,
    then add to batter.
Mix well. Shape into balls and roll in white sugar.
Place on parchment-paper lined pan and bake for
    10 minutes (longer for large cookies).
Let cool on pan until they settle—cookies will flatten
    and appear cracked.

Makes 4 dozen regular-sized cookies or 18 extravagant-
    sized cookies.

Acknowledgments

Many thanks to my wise and wonderful editor, Ann Featherstone, and to Gail Winskill and the fantastic team at Pajama Press—working with all of you is a dream come true. Thank you also to those who provided feedback during this story's early stages, and special thanks to Kip Wilson Rechea and Beth Smith for their love and support, and for helping me more than they know. I am indebted to Kristen Pranzl, Erin Bentley, Carli Bolen, and Monte Hardy for sharing their time and thoughts with me—thank you! And thank you to Jenna Beacom, Master of Deaf Education, for reviewing the manuscript—I very much appreciate your input. Finally, much love and gratitude to my family, and especially to Skip, who shares my belief in the power of stories.